A catalogue record for this book is available from the British Library

Published by Ladybird Books Ltd
A subsidiary of the Penguin Group
A Pearson Company
LADYBIRD and the device of a Ladybird are trademarks of Ladybird Books Ltd Loughborough Leicestershire UK

Disney's

THE

LION KING

Ladybird

The sun rose high in the sky and beat down on the plains of Africa.

Through the shimmering heat came birds and animals of all shapes and sizes —
from the smallest ant to the mightiest elephant. Giraffes, antelope, zebras — all were
hurrying towards Pride Rock, to welcome Prince Simba, the newborn son of
Mufasa, the Lion King, and Queen Sarabi.

A buzz of excitement ran through the crowd of animals gathered at the base of Pride Rock. Rafiki, a mystic, old baboon, began the slow steep climb to the top.

Above his head fluttered a blue-feathered hornbill. The bird, who was the King's adviser, circled twice above the crowd, then flew straight to the summit. He landed at the feet of a magnificent lion. "King Mufasa," reported the hornbill to his master, "everyone is here."

The King nodded. "Thank you, Zazu," he replied.

At last Rafiki's long climb came to an end. Silence fell as the baboon approached Queen Sarabi and the sleepy cub, nestling comfortably in her paws.

Rafiki smiled. "He looks exactly like you did when you were a cub," he told Mufasa. Rafiki blessed the new Prince then carried him to the edge of Pride Rock.

The animals below shouted and cheered, "Welcome Prince Simba, our future king!"

* * *

But not everyone was pleased with Simba's arrival. Scar, the King's brother, was jealous of Simba, for he wanted to become king himself. Mufasa went in search of Scar to ask him why he had missed the ceremony. But Scar refused to answer and stalked away, angrily.

The days passed quickly for Simba, who was a happy, lively cub.

One morning, Simba went on a long walk with his father through the vast Pride Lands.

"Look, Simba," said Mufasa. "All around you, as far as the eye can see, lies our kingdom. One day you will rule over it all."

Simba's eyes widened. "Do you think I'll be a good king, Father?" he asked.

Mufasa looked at his son. "You will if you remember that everything around us exists in a delicate balance – a great Circle of Life. You must take your place as king in that Circle and help to keep the balance."

Simba looked at the horizon. "What's that dark place over there?" he asked.

"It lies beyond our borders," said Mufasa. "You must never go there."

Just then Zazu arrived with news that some hyenas had been spotted on the Pride Lands. Whilst Mufasa went to investigate, Zazu took Simba home.

Back at Pride Rock, Simba found his uncle snoozing in the shade.

"Guess what, Uncle Scar," cried Simba. "My father just showed me the whole kingdom – and one day I'll rule it all!"

Scar thought for a minute. Then he said slyly, "Did he show you the land beyond the northern border?"

"Well, no," admitted Simba. "He said I can't go there."

"Quite right," said Scar. "An elephant graveyard is *much* too dangerous for a young prince. Only the *bravest* of lions would go there!"

An elephant graveyard! It sounded exciting. Simba raced off at once to tell Nala, his best friend.

The two young cubs went out playing together. They scampered onto the plain, talking and giggling. Simba told Nala his exciting news about the elephant graveyard. As they raced ahead towards the forbidden place, they soon managed to lose Zazu, who had been sent to keep an eye on them.

The elephant graveyard lay shrouded in mist giving it an eerie atmosphere.

Simba tried hard to be brave. "Come on, Nala," he urged, heading towards a huge elephant skull. "I think something's in there."

At that moment, Zazu fluttered down beside them. He was *very* angry. "You must leave here *immediately*," he squawked. "We are all in great danger."

Suddenly three drooling hyenas emerged from the elephant skull.

Scar had ordered the hyenas to lay in wait in the graveyard to trap and kill the cubs.

Shenzi, a female hyena, circled Zazu. "You work for Mufasa," she said.

A second hyena, Banzai, approached Simba. "So you must be…" he began.

"The future King," said Simba, trying to sound as brave as possible.

"Do you know what we do with kings who step out of their kingdoms?" Shenzi asked Simba. "We have them for – dinner!"

Terrified, Simba and Nala fled and took refuge in a gigantic rib cage. Simba felt his heart beating wildly. He took a deep breath and tried to roar. But all he could produce was a squeaky rumble.

Ed, the third hyena laughed hysterically. Shenzi began to tease Simba. "Do it again, kitty, kitty."

Simba took another deep breath.

"ROAAARRR!"

The three hyenas spun round. They looked straight into the eyes of King Mufasa. He roared again, and Shenzi, Banzai and Ed fled howling into the mist.

Later, when they were alone, Mufasa told Simba how disappointed he was. "You disobeyed me," he said.

Simba hung his head in shame. "I was just trying to be brave like you," he mumbled. Simba knew he'd let his father down.

"I'm only brave when I have to be," replied Mufasa, gently.

"But you're not scared of *anything*," said Simba.

"I was scared today," said his father. "I thought I might lose you. Just remember, being brave doesn't mean you go looking for trouble."

The sun was setting. Soon a full moon appeared, and stars twinkled in the blackening sky.

"We'll always be together, won't we, Father?" asked Simba.

Mufasa stopped. "Look up at the sky," he said.

Simba gazed upwards.

"The great kings of the past look down at us from the stars. Whenever you feel alone just remember they'll always be there to guide you – and so will I."

Simba nodded. "I'll remember," he promised.

The next morning Simba followed Scar down to the bottom of a deep, wide gorge.

"Wait here," Scar told Simba. "Your father has a marvellous surprise for you." He turned to leave. "Now I'll go and tell him you're ready." Scar sauntered away, leaving his nephew all alone.

The hyenas were waiting at the entrance to the gorge. When Scar gave the signal they ran towards a herd of wildebeest forcing them to stampede in Simba's direction. The terrified cub clawed his way up onto the branch of a fallen tree.

Scar's plan was working perfectly. He ran to his brother's side. "Mufasa!" he called. "Quick! There's a stampede. Simba's trapped!"

Mufasa leapt into the gorge, grabbed Simba in his mouth and carried him to safety. However as he was climbing out of the gorge, Mufasa was knocked backwards by the galloping wildebeest.

Injured and in pain, he struggled to pull himself onto an overhanging rock. Slowly he looked up to see Scar leaning over him. "Help me," pleaded Mufasa.

Scar dug his claws into his brother's paws. "Long live the King," he snarled, pushing Mufasa back down into the path of the stampeding wildebeest.

When the dust finally settled, Scar found Simba sobbing over the body of his dead father.

"This is all *your* fault," Scar lied to Simba. "If it weren't for you, he'd still be alive. You must leave the Pride and *never* return."

Heartbroken, Simba fled. He staggered on until eventually, hot and exhausted, he collapsed in the desert. Hungry vultures began to circle overhead.

Meanwhile Scar had returned to Pride Rock and proclaimed himself as the new King. He told Sarabi that both Mufasa and Simba were dead.

But Simba was still alive! When he finally opened his eyes, Simba found a skinny meerkat and a fat warthog gazing down at him.

"My name is Timon," said the meerkat, "and this is Pumbaa."

"I have to go," said Simba, rising shakily to his feet.

"Where to?" asked Timon.

"I don't know," sighed Simba miserably. "I can't go back home, I've done something terrible."

"Then put your past behind you," said Timon, "and stay with us in the jungle. Take our advice – *hakuna matata* – no worries!"

Simba thought for a moment. He had nowhere else to go. "All right," he agreed.

"Good!" exclaimed Timon. "Now you must be hungry. Try this!"

Simba looked at the fat grub squirming in Timon's paw. It looked disgusting, but he was very hungry so he tried it. It tasted surprisingly good. Perhaps life in the jungle wouldn't be too bad after all!

The years passed by and Simba grew into a handsome young lion.

One starry night Simba lay thinking. He was imagining what his father would think of him now. He sighed deeply and his breath scattered a puff of milkweed into the air.

A sudden wind sprang up and carried the milkweed far away into the outstretched hand of Rafiki. The old baboon examined the seeds and hobbled into his cave to study a picture of a lion cub he had once painted.

Rafiki opened a gourd and smeared the sticky liquid around the cub's head. The picture changed into the image of a lion, with a golden mane.

Rafiki smiled and prepared to leave for the jungle.

*　*　*

The next day Timon and Pumbaa were out hunting for bugs when Simba heard them cry and shout for help. He rushed to their aid and rescued them from a hungry lioness. As the lioness wrestled him to the ground, Simba looked at her closely and suddenly recognised who she was – it was Nala!

The two friends were delighted to see each other again. Simba introduced Nala to his friends and then took her on a tour of the jungle.

"It's just like paradise," said Nala, "but Simba you must return home. Things are terrible there since Scar took over the Pride Lands. He lets the hyenas do whatever they want," she said. "Accept your responsibilities – you are the rightful King."

"I'm not fit to be king," said Simba sadly, and he turned and walked away.

That night Simba lay thinking about what Nala had said. Suddenly Simba heard a noise. He looked up and saw Rafiki. The old baboon led him to a small pool. The clouds parted and Mufasa's image filled the sky.

"Simba," said the voice of Mufasa, "you are my son, and the one true King. You must take your place in the Circle of Life."

Simba knew at once that he must return to the Pride Lands.

* * *

Meanwhile, all had not been well at Pride Rock. Stocks were low and the hyenas were hungry.

"It's the lionesses' job to hunt for food," snapped Scar. "Sarabi, where is your hunting party?"

"There is nothing left to hunt," said Sarabi. "We must all leave Pride Rock, or we will die of hunger."

"We're not going anywhere!" roared Scar. "I am the King, and I make the rules."

Suddenly a mighty roar filled the air. Scar turned round to see Simba.

"I've come back to take my place as the true King," said Simba.

Scar signalled to the pack of hyenas. Instantly they swarmed towards Simba. Caught off balance, Simba was pushed backwards, and he slipped over the cliff's edge. He struggled to cling to the crumbling rock.

"You look just the way your father did before I killed him," sneered Scar.

Scar's words filled Simba with new strength. He leapt up and knocked Scar aside.

Scar called to the hyenas to save him, but Nala and the lionesses drove them back.

A sudden flash of lightning ignited the dry grass around Pride Rock. As the fire blazed on all sides, Simba lunged at Scar, knocking him over the steep edge of the cliff to his death below.

"Welcome home," said Nala, as she smiled and nuzzled Simba. "Your mother is waiting to greet the new King."

As the whole Pride celebrated Simba's victory, the rain began to fall, putting out the flames and soaking the black, smoky ground. Within minutes, sheets of water drenched the plains, and gurgling streams snaked across the land once again.

With the arrival of the rain the Pride Lands came back to life. Green shoots sprang up from the fire blackened earth and the herds returned once more to graze on the plains.

*   *   *

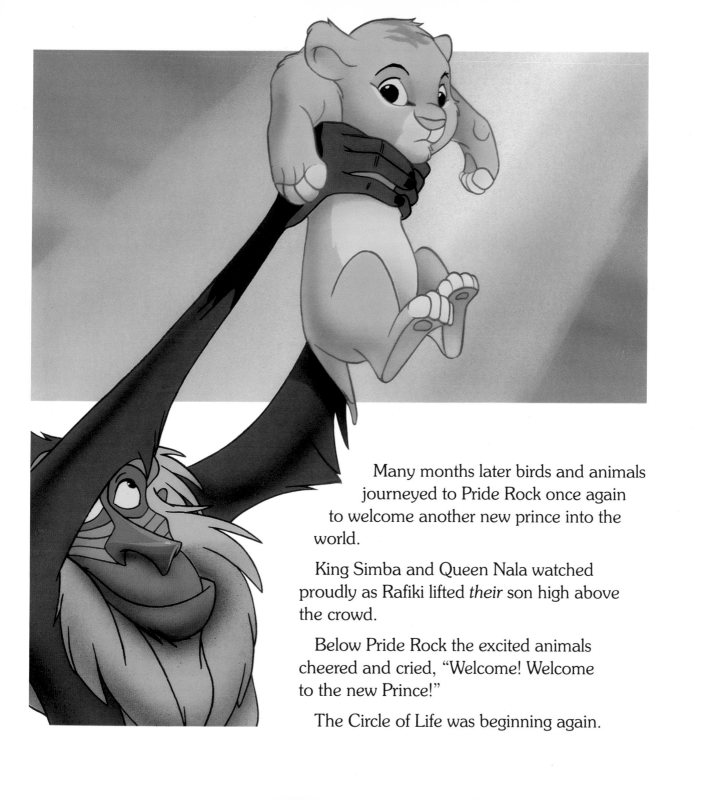

Many months later birds and animals journeyed to Pride Rock once again to welcome another new prince into the world.

King Simba and Queen Nala watched proudly as Rafiki lifted *their* son high above the crowd.

Below Pride Rock the excited animals cheered and cried, "Welcome! Welcome to the new Prince!"

The Circle of Life was beginning again.